WELCOME TO
PASSPORT TO READING
A beginning reader's ticket to a brand-new world!

Every book in this program is designed to build read-along and read-alone skills, level by level, through engaging and enriching stories. As the reader turns each page, he or she will become more confident with new vocabulary, sight words, and comprehension.

These PASSPORT TO READING levels will help you choose the perfect book for every reader.

READING TOGETHER
Read short words in simple sentence structures together to begin a reader's journey.

READING OUT LOUD
Encourage developing readers to sound out words in more complex stories with simple vocabulary.

READING INDEPENDENTLY
Newly independent readers gain confidence reading more complex sentences with higher word counts.

READY TO READ MORE
Readers prepare for chapter books with fewer illustrations and longer paragraphs.

This book features sight words from the educator-supported Dolch Sight Words List. This encourages the reader to recognize commonly used vocabulary words, increasing reading speed and fluency.

For more information, please visit passporttoreadingbooks.com.

Enjoy the journey!

Little, Brown and Company

Hachette Book Group
237 Park Avenue, New York, NY 10017
Visit our website at lb-kids.com

Little, Brown and Company is a division of Hachette Book Group, Inc. The Little, Brown name and logo are trademarks of Hachette Book Group, Inc.

The publisher is not responsible for websites (or their content) that are not owned by the publisher.

First Edition: September 2014

Library of Congress Control Number: 2013957718

ISBN 978-0-316-40557-7

10 9 8 7 6 5 4 3 2 1

CW

Printed in the United States of America

Passport to Reading titles are leveled by independent reviewers applying the standards developed by Irene Fountas and Gay Su Pinnell in *Matching Books to Readers: Using Leveled Books in Guided Reading*, Heinemann, 1999.

Licensed By:

TRANSFORMERS RESCUE BOTS

Team of Heroes

by Jennifer Fox

LITTLE, BROWN AND COMPANY
New York   Boston

Attention, Rescue Bots fans!
Look for these words when you read
this book. Can you spot them all?

Earth

human

lava

car

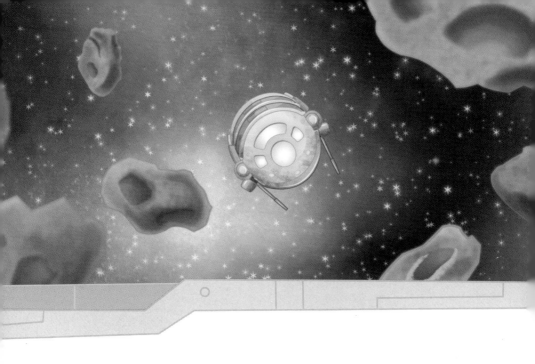

A new class of Autobots
lands on planet Earth!

They are the Rescue Bots.

Their leader, Optimus Prime, tells them their mission.

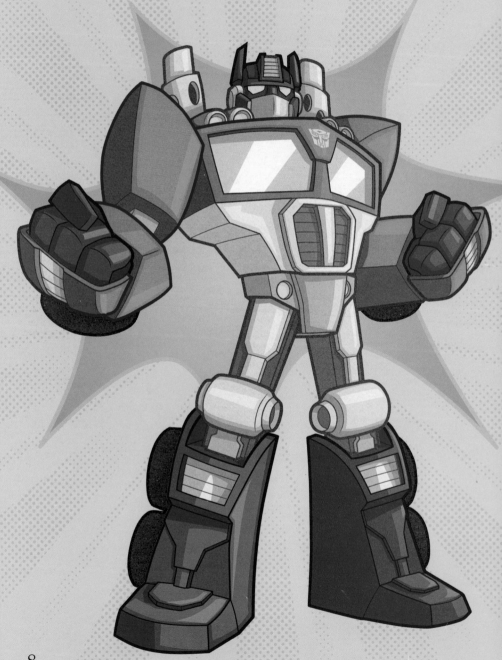

"Work together
with the humans.
Serve and protect," he says.

The Rescue Bots choose vehicle forms
that will help them
be a great rescue team.

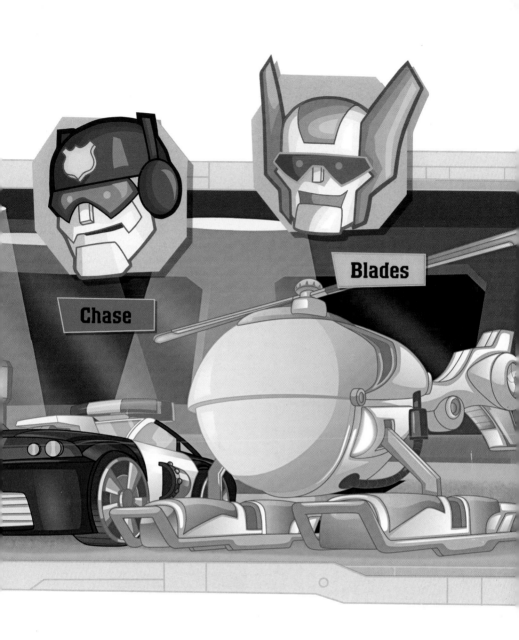

Heatwave, Boulder,
Chase, and Blades
are ready to roll out!

The Rescue Bots will work
with Chief Charlie Burns.

The human is the leader
of Griffin Rock Rescue.

Chief Burns's family will help, too.

Cody is the youngest Burns.

He is a great dispatcher.

Kade played football in school,
and now he is a firefighter.

Dani is the chief's only daughter.
She enjoys action and danger.
She is a tough pilot.

Graham is smart and steady
in any tricky situation.
He is an engineer.

Cody calls the team.
They need to gather
for a mission.

"There is trouble on the roads,"
he tells them.

"Roll to the rescue!"
Heatwave shouts.

The Rescue Bots change
into their vehicle forms.
They roll out to save
the people of Griffin Rock.

Dani and Blades fly high
to get a better look.

A bridge is out!
Kade and Heatwave
rush into action.

They save a man

from the raging river.

Boulder and Graham
find a hot problem—
a lava leak!

The town is in danger,
but the Rescue Bots
show no fear.

A car skids into
a lava puddle.

But Chase is on the scene!

He scoops up the driver, Hayley,

just in time.

The rest of the team stop the lava.

Chief Burns says, "Mission accomplished!"

The streets are safe again.

Chief Burns is proud
of his family.

He is proud of the Rescue Bots, too.

The rescue team
knows what it takes
to get the job done:
teamwork!